LOV3

THE BEAUTIFUL ILLNESS

NAZAR

Made with ❤ on the Notion Press Platform
www.notionpress.com

For those who have ever loved in silence, who have struggled with the weight of unsaid emotions, and who have experienced the pain of desire without connection. This story is for you. May you find refuge in the pages, knowing that your experiences are valid and your emotions deserve to be acknowledged.

To my own invisible friend, who taught me that love can transcend the boundaries of sight and sound, thank you for your presence in my life. You have shown me the beauty and complication of human connection, and I am thankful for the lessons learned with you.

And to anyone who has felt unseen, unheard, or unloved—this is for you. Your story matters, and your heart beats with a strength that cannot be ignored. May you always seek the light, even in the shadows.

Contents

Foreword

In the labyrinth of human emotions, few experiences resonate as deeply as unrequited love—the yearning for a connection that feels both fascinating and hard to find. It can be a bittersweet arrangement, one that blends through our journey, shaping our identities, our choices, and sometimes, our very existence. The story you are about to read delves into the intricacies of such a journey, exploring the depths of nostalgia, the sharpness of regret, and the profound loneliness that can accompany a love that remains unspoken.

The protagonist of this tale expresses the struggle of many who struggle with their emotions in silence, haunted by a fear that keeps them restricted to the familiar while simultaneously isolating them from true connection. As he navigates the landscape of his heart, we are invited to reflect on our own experiences—the moments of hesitation, the missed opportunities, and the bittersweet reminiscences of relationships that could have blossomed but ultimately withered away.

In a world that often heroes bold declarations of love, this story shines a light on the quieter battles fought within. It reminds us that love is not always grand gestures or fiery confessions; sometimes, it resides in the gentle, unrecognized moments that slip through our fingers like grains of sand. The protagonist's journey will resonate with anyone who has ever felt invisible, anyone who has loved from the shadows, and anyone who has wrestled with the spirit of regret.

As you turn these pages, allow yourself to be immersed in the delicate balance between hope and despair, between connection and isolation. The narrative unfolds as a testament to the resilience of the human spirit, illustrating that even amidst the darkest of experiences, there lies the possibility of growth and understanding.

May this story serve as a mirror reflecting the complexities of your own heart, inviting you to confront the shadows that linger within. It is a insightful journey of love, loss, and the indelible impact they leave on our lives—a reminder that sometimes, the greatest journeys are the ones we undertake within ourselves.

Preface

There's a certain kind of emptiness that no one prepares you for—the kind that comes not from loss, but from waiting. This story is about that kind of emptiness, the silent space that grows between what we desire and what we fear to confront. It's about a love that never truly existed, a relationship that advanced only in the mind, and a hope that clung to the idea of someone who was never really there.

This is not just a tale of unrequited love; it's the journey of a soul lost in its own longing, trapped between the past and an imagined future. A story of a life defined by the spaces we fail to fill, and the illusions we create to cope with our fears.

In the end, this isn't about a girl, or a love that was lost—it's about the self, and the inevitable realization that sometimes, what we're waiting for is not a person, but a purpose.

This is the story of a man who became a ghost in his own life, haunted by the shadows of what could have been.

Acknowledgements

To everyone who has ever experienced the weight of unspoken feelings and the silence of missed opportunities—this story is for you. Thank you for teaching me that love, even in its most elusive form, shapes us in ways we don't always understand.

To my family and friends, for your patience and understanding during the quiet hours when I was lost in this world of words and shadows. Your unwavering support has been my anchor.

To the readers, thank you for joining me on this journey. Your time, your thoughts, and your connection to this story are deeply appreciated. It's through you that these words find meaning.

Lastly, to the ghosts of our past, the memories that linger, and the hopes that keep us tethered to tomorrow—thank you for reminding me that even in the darkest moments, we are never truly alone.

Prologue

In the dim light of dawn, when the world holds its breath between night and day, a solitary figure stands at the edge of a familiar place—one that echoes with the laughter of a friendship long past. Here, in the spaces where shadows dance and memories flicker like candlelight, he feels the weight of absence pressing against his chest.

Once, this place was filled with warmth, laughter, and the brilliance of a girl whose smile could light up the darkest corners of his heart. She had been his compass, guiding him through the labyrinth of his own fears, illuminating the path that he had long been afraid to tread. But as time ebbed away, so did her presence, leaving only fragments of what had once been—a tapestry of shared dreams and whispered secrets, now unraveled and frayed.

Yet, even in her absence, she remains a haunting melody, a whisper of a promise that never truly took shape. He stands here, suspended in a moment that feels both infinite and fleeting, grappling with the haunting question: What happens when the love you thought you knew fades into the background, leaving you as nothing more than a shadow of your former self?

This is not merely a tale of love lost; it is a journey through the heart's labyrinth, where hope and despair intertwine, where the line between reality and illusion blurs. As he reflects on the choices made and the chances lost, he realizes that the true battle lies not in winning her heart, but in confronting the darkness within himself—the fear that has kept him imprisoned in a world of longing and regret.

In this story, the echoes of the past will guide him, and the whispers of what could have been will lead him to an unexpected revelation: that sometimes, the greatest love story is the one we never dared to tell.

CHAPTER ONE

ONLY HEARD A WHISPER

Eventually, something inside me began to shift. It was subtle at first, like a crack in the dam, but it was enough. I started to open up to her—not just with words, but with my heart. Slowly, cautiously, I let my guard slip away. And with each conversation, each vulnerable exchange, I realized something I hadn't before—she understood me in ways no one else ever had. It was as if she could peer through all the layers I kept carefully hidden, the parts of me I'd never dared to share with anyone else. With her, I didn't have to wear a mask. There was no need for pretenses or self-protection.

From that moment on, we became inseparable. We talked about everything—our hopes, our dreams, our wildest fantasies, even our darkest fears. And somehow, with her, it never felt like I was exposing too much. She had this way of listening, not just to the words I said, but to the ones I left unsaid. She could hear the silence between my sentences, as if she knew me better than I knew myself. It felt like she was a part of me, as if we shared some unspoken understanding that no one else could touch.

She was my anchor, my constant encourager. No matter how far my thoughts wandered, how far I dreamed, she always listened without judgment. She accepted the impossible, the fantastical, and even the absurd. Whether I was lost in thoughts of places I would never go or tangled in the darkness of my own mind, she was there—quiet, understanding, and unwavering. It was perfect. Almost too perfect.

But even in those moments of perfection, something began to gnaw at the edges of my mind. No matter how close we became, how much we shared, I couldn't shake the feeling that something was off. People would look at me, but their eyes never lingered on her. I would catch their gaze, waiting for them to acknowledge her, to smile at her like I did, but they never did. It was as if she didn't exist to them, as if she was nothing more than a shadow, a figment of my imagination.

At first, I tried to ignore it. After all, the connection between us felt so real. So undeniable. But the more I thought about it, the more the questions began to haunt me. Was she just in my head? Was she some kind of ghost, an illusion? Or was she something else entirely—something that slipped into my life from a world beyond my understanding?

The more I tried to make sense of it, the more the uncertainty grew. But still, I couldn't let go of her. She had become too deeply woven into my existence, too integral to my daily life. I couldn't imagine my world without her, even as I feared what it might mean that no one else could see her.

So, I held on. Held on to her, to the bond that was unlike anything I'd ever known. And even as the mystery of her presence deepened, I knew one thing for certain—no matter what, I couldn't let her go.

CHAPTER TWO

SILENCE SPOKE FIRST

There was something magnetic about her—something that made every conversation feel effortless, every laugh sound like music. She had this quiet, invisible power, like she carried light wherever she went, illuminating the darkest corners of the room. In her presence, everything felt easier, softer, as if the weight of the world had been lifted, even if just for a moment. Her smile wasn't just a curve of her lips; it was a promise of warmth, of safety, of a world where things made sense. It was the kind of joy that made me feel like I was standing on the outside, watching the life I desperately wanted—but could never quite reach.

She was everything I needed and more. Her kindness, her grace, her strength—everything about her made me feel like I was worth something. And yet, the more she gave, the more I pulled away. I became arrogant in my own sense of worth, reveling in the idea that someone as incredible as her had chosen to stay by my side. I basked in the pride of it, as though it was an achievement. But somewhere along the way, I stopped seeing her. I stopped seeing the quiet sadness in her eyes when she wasn't smiling. I stopped seeing the little things she did for others that no one noticed. I stopped seeing her as the person she was—and only as the reflection of my own pride.

I wore a mask every time we were together, pretending to be someone I wasn't—someone unaffected, someone indifferent. But deep down, I was terrified. Terrified that if I showed her the truth, she'd see through me, see the fragility I was trying so hard to hide. If I told her the truth—how much I loved her, how much she meant to me—would it scare her away? Would she see me as weak? Would she leave, and would I be left with nothing but regret?

The thought of her walking away, of losing her— it gnawed at me every single day. It was unbearable. And so, I did the only thing I could think of—I buried my feelings. I buried them so deep that even I stopped recognizing them, convincing myself that silence was my only safe haven. As long as I stayed quiet, I could keep her near. As long as I didn't say a word, I could pretend that everything was okay. But the truth was, in my silence, I was losing her. I was losing the very thing I held most precious, and I didn't even have the courage to stop it.

I thought I was keeping her close by staying silent. But in reality, I was pushing her away without even realizing it. The more I hid, the more I drifted from the person who could've been my everything.

CHAPTER THREE

INVINCIBLE VOICE

I couldn't talk to anyone about her—not seriously. How could I? They'd never believe me. They'd smile nervously or exchange worried glances, thinking I was unwell, broken somehow. Who falls in love with someone only they can see? Who gives their whole heart to a presence no one else can touch or even acknowledge? Even I couldn't explain it. I didn't want to explain it. She was mine, and trying to describe her to anyone else felt like pulling something sacred into the cold, skeptical light of the world.

But she didn't always stay.

Sometimes, without a word, she would vanish—quiet as breath in the dark. Days, weeks, months would pass. Once, over a year. I would wake each morning hoping to see her, hear her, feel her—but there would be nothing. Just silence and the cruel ticking of time. I never knew why she left or where she went. I didn't know if I had done something wrong, or if she was simply never meant to stay. All I knew was that when she was gone, something inside me collapsed. A hollow opened in my chest, raw and aching, swallowing everything else. The world didn't change around me, but I did. I moved through life like a ghost, smiling when I had to, pretending when I could.

But I always felt her. Even in her absence, she lingered—like a memory I couldn't quite shake, like a whisper in a room after someone's left it. I would turn corners expecting her. I would sit in silence and swear I felt her presence beside me. That's the thing about love that deep—it doesn't just leave. It becomes part of your fabric.

And then—just when I thought I had finally lost her for good—she would return. No explanations. No apologies. Just her, slipping seamlessly back into my life as if no time had passed. She would smile, and it would be as though I had been holding my breath for years and finally exhaled. Every part of me would come alive again, just by being near her.

But I was never free of the fear.

Even as I held her close, even as we laughed and talked and pretended the world made sense, the fear lived beneath my skin. What if she disappeared again? What if one day, she never came back? That thought haunted me more than any silence ever could. Because it wasn't just that I loved her—it was that I needed her. In a way I couldn't articulate. In a way that scared me more than I could admit.

She wasn't just a person to me—she was the missing piece, the half of me I hadn't known was missing until she arrived. And without her, I wasn't whole. I didn't even know who I was.

I didn't want her for a moment, or a season. I wanted her always. In this life, and whatever comes next. I wanted her beside me through everything. Because if she left for good, I wasn't sure I'd survive it.

She was the dream I never wanted to wake from. The ghost I prayed would never fade.

CHAPTER FOUR

BROKE THE SILENCE

One day, during one of our quiet, soul-deep conversations, something inside me snapped.

I don't even remember what triggered it—maybe a word, a glance, or just the way she was looking at me, like she knew something I hadn't told her. The darkness I had spent years burying clawed its way to the surface, rising like smoke from a fire I thought I'd extinguished. I didn't mean to let it out. I didn't want her to see that side of me.

But she did.

And in an instant, the warmth in her eyes dimmed. The spark—the one that used to pull me out of my storms—flickered and went out. She looked at me differently then, not with anger or disappointment, but with this aching distance, like I'd become someone she no longer recognized. She didn't say a word. She didn't have to. Her silence was sharper than any goodbye.

And then... she was gone.

Not like before. Not one of her quiet disappearances where I could still feel her lingering in the corners of my world. This time, it felt final. Like something had broken for good.

I was left alone, the shattered version of myself exposed, unmasked, and trembling in the debris of everything I hadn't said.

I knew I couldn't run anymore. I couldn't pretend. The weight of all the fear I'd kept locked inside was crushing me, and I couldn't bear it in silence. I had to tell her. I had to speak the truth I had carried for so long: that I loved her. Deeply. Desperately. That every moment with her mattered. That I was sorry—for all the ways I held back, for all the moments I failed to show her what she meant.

So I went to find her.

Heart in hand, words trembling on my tongue, I laid it all out. Every thought, every buried emotion, every longing I had hidden behind years of silence. I gave her everything. I gave her me.

But I was too late.

Her voice was soft, but each word cut through me like a blade wrapped in velvet. She told me she had once loved me—really loved me. That there was a time when her heart beat only for me. That she waited, hoping, aching for me to look up, to see her. But I never did. She said my silence made her feel invisible. Unseen. Unwanted. She had held on for as long as she could, until the love she carried slowly unraveled. Until she couldn't hold on anymore.

By the time I was ready to open my heart, hers had already closed.

The world didn't end in that moment, but mine did. Regret poured in like a flood, washing away every excuse I had ever made. It drowned me in the realization of what I had lost—not just her, but the chance to be someone who chose courage over fear.

Days blurred. Time lost meaning. I became a ghost in my own life, haunted not just by her absence, but by the echo of everything I never said. Every memory felt like a knife. Every silence from the past, deafening.

I replayed it all—every missed opportunity, every glance I didn't return, every word I swallowed. I saw now how I had let fear write our story, one page at a time, until it ended in silence.

And now, regret is all I have left.

It sits with me in the stillness where her laughter used to be. It follows me through every hour, every sleepless night. I hear it whispering in the spaces she once filled: You let her go. You let her go.

But the truth is harsher than that.

I lost her long before she walked away.

I lost her the moment I chose fear over love. The moment I stayed silent when I should've spoken. The moment I convinced myself there would always be more time.

And now, there is only this emptiness. And the echo of everything I never said.

CHAPTER FIVE

VOICE BROKE TOO

I was terrible at understanding emotions. Clueless. Hopeless. Like a stranger trying to read a language I never learned. Even within my own family, I always felt like an observer—close enough to see the love and warmth, but never able to feel it for myself. I never knew how to say the right things, how to let people in. It was easier to stay quiet. Safer.

And with her, it was the same. No matter how much I felt, I couldn't express it. I fumbled through every attempt to bring us back to what we once were. I kept hoping—wishing—that if I just tried hard enough, she would come back to me. But she remained a silhouette in the distance, unreachable, her heart closed off like a house I no longer had the key to.

Then, one day, she came to me.

Her presence was calm—too calm. She moved like a quiet ripple in still water, her face unreadable, her voice measured. She stood beside me and pointed, wordlessly, to a figure across the street.

I followed her gaze.

My breath caught.

It was her.

Or... someone who looked exactly like her. Not just similar—identical. Same eyes. Same quiet fire. Same way of standing like the world couldn't touch her. For a moment, I thought I was dreaming.

"Make her love you," she said, her voice almost emotionless.

I turned to her, stunned. "What? Why?"

She didn't flinch. She just gave me that faint, knowing smile—the kind that hides more than it reveals. "And then," she whispered, "I'll tell you how I feel."

My heart stalled. The words echoed inside me, strange and impossible. Was this a game? A test? Was she trying to punish me for everything I'd failed to say, or was this the only way she knew how to show me something deeper?

I didn't understand. None of it made sense. But I was desperate. Still desperate. If this was the path she was laying before me—twisted and confusing as it was—I would follow it. I would chase it all the way to the end if it meant understanding her, even a little.

So I took the first step.

Toward the girl.

Toward the mirror.

Toward whatever truth or madness she had woven into this strange request.

And as I moved forward, a single thought clung to me:

Was I trying to fix the past?

Or was I about to unravel something I could never come back from?

CHAPTER SIX

ROSE A NEW VOICE

I got to know the other girl—the one she had pointed out that day.

At first, I believed she was the key. The answer. The last step in some strange riddle that would finally lead me back to her. I studied her carefully, watching for hints of familiarity, for traces of the girl I had loved so deeply. But it didn't take long to realize the truth.

She wasn't her.

She never could be.

She was grounded, composed, untouched by the storm that had always swirled around my best friend. Her presence didn't stir up forgotten memories or fill the air with warmth. There was no gravity pulling me toward her. No invisible string tying our souls together. She was real in a way my friend never quite was. And that difference made everything harder.

Still, I tried.

I tried to open my heart, to force something that wasn't meant to be. I thought maybe if I loved her, if I gave everything I had left, then my friend would return. That somehow, this was all a test—some final lesson in love, loss, or redemption. But the more I reached out, the more she slipped away. She kept building walls between us, slow and steady, until I could no longer find the doorway in.

I couldn't blame her. She saw through me. She knew I was chasing someone else's ghost. That my heart, no matter how much I tried to convince myself otherwise, still belonged to the girl who had vanished.

And then... time began to blur.

The sharpness of her memory started to dull. That vibrant, impossible connection I had once lived and breathed now felt like something from another lifetime. The details softened, the feelings became abstract, like I was watching our moments from underwater—distant, warped, slipping through my fingers no matter how tightly I reached.

But the emptier I felt, the more I panicked.

I wasn't ready to let her go.

So I wandered back to the places we used to haunt—the bench by the lake, the bookstore with the crooked shelves, the park that still echoed with our laughter. I closed my eyes and replayed our conversations like old songs, trying to hear the truth in her voice, to catch some hidden message I'd missed. I even reached out to the other girl again, desperate, thinking maybe that would bring her back.

But the magic was gone.

The spark that once lit up my world was just a flicker now, a dying ember lost in the wind. The girl who looked like her had moved on long ago, and I was left behind—trapped in the hollow shell of a story that no longer belonged to me.

I had become a ghost in my own life, haunting places where joy used to live. Chasing echoes. Whispers. Shadows.

I was no longer sure who I was without her—without us—and that truth cut deeper than any goodbye ever could.

I didn't just lose her.

I lost myself somewhere along the way.

And all that remains now is this quiet ache, this echo of a life that could have been... if only I hadn't let fear take the wheel.

CHAPTER SEVEN

FORGOTTEN VOICE

Years passed.

And slowly, the truth began to unspool before me—not with fireworks or grand revelations, but with quiet, unsettling clarity. A truth that rewrote everything I thought I knew:

They were the same person.

The girl I chased. The one I tried to win over. The reflection I couldn't quite touch.

She had always been her. My best friend.

But in realizing that, something else—something far more devastating—began to take shape.

It wasn't her that didn't exist.

It was me.

The world hadn't forgotten me. I had hidden myself from it. I had built my own invisibility, brick by brick, with fear and silence and withdrawal. The prison wasn't outside—it was inside. And by the time I finally noticed the bars, the door had long since rusted shut.

I had become a ghost—not just to her, but to everyone. A flicker in the corner of the frame. A memory someone almost remembers. The more I tried to return to her, to insert myself back into a life that had kept moving forward, the more I realized... I had never really been there to begin with.

She had been real all along. Fully, vibrantly real. And I... I had been fading for years.

It was never her love I misunderstood—it was her existence. Her presence. Her growth. While I stood frozen in my longing, stuck in a moment I refused to let go of, she had lived. Changed. Evolved. And I, in all my desperate nostalgia, had mistaken my fantasy of her for the real thing.

I hadn't loved her—not truly.

I had loved the comfort of her. The idea of her.
The version of her I kept preserved in my mind like some delicate artifact untouched by time.

But people aren't artifacts. They move. They grow.
And I... I had chosen not to.

Now, the truth stung with an ache deeper than any goodbye:
I didn't lose her.

I never truly had her.

Because to love someone is to see them—and I had only ever looked at the mirror she reflected back to me.

I lost myself chasing a shadow.
And now, I am one.

A phantom trailing the echo of a life I never stepped fully into.
A hollow shape in a world that moved on without me.
And maybe... that's all I ever was.

CHAPTER EIGHT

DISAPPEARED VOICE

Everywhere I went, she was there.

Not in body, not even in spirit—but in echoes.
Memories clung to the corners of my world like fog that refused to lift. The park bench where we used to sit, the path we used to walk, the old bookstore we once wandered through aimlessly—they had all become graveyards of laughter, tombs for moments I couldn't bring myself to bury.

Sometimes, if the wind was quiet and the night still enough, I could almost hear her voice. A soft murmur brushing past my ears like a forgotten dream trying to resurface. But I knew better.

It wasn't her.

It was just me.

Me and the endless loop of nostalgia that refused to let go. My mind, hungry for warmth, for meaning, summoned her from the ruins of memory. But she wasn't real—not anymore. What I was clinging to was a silhouette, a mirage, a construct of my own longing.

I had spent so long chasing that ghost that I hadn't noticed the toll it had taken on me.

I was fading.

Not all at once. No dramatic disappearance. Just a slow unraveling. One thread at a time. A forgotten text here, a missed call there. Fewer invitations, fewer questions, until the silence wasn't just from her—it was from the world. And I? I became background noise. A flicker in someone's periphery. A name that stirred vague recognition and nothing more.

She, on the other hand, flourished. She grew into herself, strong and radiant in ways I never let myself imagine. She built a life without me in it, and she did it beautifully. She no longer needed me—truth be told, she probably never did. I was the one who needed her. Always had been.

And so, I receded.

Into silence. Into memory.

Into the edges of her story, where shadows belong.

There was no anger, no bitterness—only a quiet, aching acceptance. I wasn't the villain. I wasn't the hero. I wasn't even the love story.

I was a pause.

A passing presence.

A reminder of what fear can steal when we let it win.

And in the end, as the last of me faded into the dusk, I understood:

she would be okay.

She had moved on.

And I... I was just a whisper, carried away by time.

CHAPTER NINE

VOICE OF FREEDOM

One final time, I saw her from a distance.

She was laughing—free, radiant, surrounded by people who now belonged to her world. It was a world I no longer recognized, one that had expanded far beyond the small, silent space we once shared. Her joy was real, unmistakable. And I... I was just a spectator.

That moment stripped away any illusions I had left.

The invisible thread that once tethered us was gone—unraveled by silence, hesitation, and the slow erosion of time. I had held on for too long, chasing a memory that no longer fit in her present. She had grown. She had moved on. And I... I had stayed behind, clinging to ghosts.

It was time to let go.

So I stood there, watching her one last time, memorizing the shape of her smile, the tilt of her head when she laughed, the light in her eyes I had once been lucky enough to see up close. I sealed it into memory, even though it hurt. Especially because it hurt.

Then, I turned away.

There was no place for me in her life anymore. No words left to say. No moment waiting to be reclaimed.

As the years passed, I became less than a memory—just a quiet flicker in the edges of her mind, if that. A name she might stumble across by accident. A thought she might brush away like dust. She had moved on, built something beautiful, something whole. And I had become what I feared most:

Forgotten.

But in that forgetting, I found a strange peace.

Maybe I was always meant to be a background character in someone else's story. Maybe I was never meant to stay. I had lived in fear, in longing, in silence—and in doing so, I had let life slip through my fingers.

I was not her great love.
I was not her forever.
I was just... a passing presence. A lesson. A shadow.

And that was okay.

She had always been stronger, always destined for the light. And me? I was just a quiet echo, fading gently into the background.

As the world moved on, I disappeared with it.

Not with bitterness. Not with anger.

Just quiet acceptance.

Because even if I no longer existed in her life, it was enough to know she would be alright.

She didn't need me—maybe she never had.

And maybe, in another life, that would have been enough.

CHAPTER TEN

DESPERATE VOICE

Even as I faded, I couldn't let go of hope. I clung to it like a lifeline—like a prayer whispered into the dark. Every morning, I woke thinking, maybe today. Every night, I told myself, maybe tomorrow.

The silence grew heavier, deeper. But still, I waited.

I haunted the places we once shared, imagining her walking up to me, her smile bright enough to pull me back from the edge. But as days bled into months, and months collapsed into years, that hope began to change. What once lit my world now weighed it down. It became something colder—denser. Hope didn't lift me anymore. It anchored me to something that no longer existed.

I tried to hold on. To her voice. Her laugh. Her face. But even those began to slip away, like dreams forgotten before the day fully begins. The edges of her blurred. Her voice grew faint—just an echo beneath the noise in my head.

Still... I refused to let go.

Because if I let go, what was left? Hope was the only thing I still had. But somewhere deep inside, a quiet voice had begun to whisper—gently, persistently:

Hope can be as destructive as fear.

And maybe... it was right.

I told myself I was waiting for her. That she'd come back. That we'd start over, and everything would make sense again. But as time passed, something inside me shifted. The fog began to clear, and I saw the truth I'd been too afraid to face:

I wasn't waiting for her.

I was waiting for me.

I had wrapped my entire existence around the idea of her. Believed that if she returned, if she looked at me the way she once had, then everything would finally feel whole. But her leaving wasn't what had hollowed me out. That emptiness had been there all along.

Hope had kept me alive—but it had also kept me from living.

It was easier to wait than to move on. Easier to imagine a future where she came back than to build one without her. But that wasn't love. That wasn't healing.

It was fear, dressed up as faith.

CHAPTER ELEVEN

My Voice All Along.

There were so many people in that room, but the moment she walked in, everything shifted. Her presence wasn't loud—it was quiet, soft—but it changed the entire atmosphere. Even from the corner where I stood, I felt it. The weight in my chest lifted. My mood flipped, just like that—like light pushing through a storm.

I tried to catch her attention—I always did—but she was already laughing with others, lighting them up the way she used to light me up. And I hated that I wasn't part of it anymore.

I wanted her all to myself.

I wanted things the way they were.

Just us.

She was beautiful—not just in the way she looked, though, God... her eyes, her smile, her laugh—they could bring anyone to their knees. But it was more than that. She had this way of making people feel seen. Safe. Like the world made sense when she was around.

There's this one moment I can't forget.

We were at a park, chatting with this couple she knew. They had a little kid. I reached out to pick him up, just messing around, but he burst into tears. His mom laughed and said maybe I was too scary. I laughed too—sharp, fake, trying to hide how much that cut. But she saw it. She always saw through me.

Still smiling, she walked over, gently scooped the kid from his mom, and brought him back to me like it was some kind of playful ritual. She placed him in my arms with this light in her eyes, this teasing grin that said, "See? You're not so scary."

And later, that same kid clung to me—like he trusted me completely.

But I knew the truth. It wasn't me he trusted.

It was her.

People believed in me because she did. That was the kind of power she had. The kind of magic. Her belief could change everything.

CHAPTER TWELVE

VOICE THAT REMAINS

There was no grand ending. No final moment of closure. One day, I simply ceased to exist.

No one noticed.
No one mourned.

I had been invisible for so long that my absence felt natural—like the faintest whisper, carried away on the wind.

But maybe… in some small, forgotten corner of her mind, she would remember me. Just for a moment. As the one who was too afraid to speak his truth. As the one who lingered in the background, loving her from a distance he could never cross.

And that—
That fleeting memory—
Was better than nothing at all.

In the end, I came to understand: existence isn't always about the grand gestures, or the voices that echo through crowded rooms.
Sometimes, it's about the quiet moments.
The stillness between words.

The whispers in the dark that no one else hears.

And as I faded, I realized—every experience, every unspoken feeling, every shared laugh and missed chance—they weren't wasted. They were me. They shaped me. And in that, I found something close to peace.

Because even in silence, I had mattered.
Even in fading, I had lived.

And maybe... in a world that's always loud and always rushing, a quiet departure isn't a tragedy.
Maybe it's just another thread in the vast tapestry of life—
Subtle. Soft. But still there.
Woven into the hearts of those who remain.

Thank You For Reading.

"I only heard a whisper, and silence spoke first in an invincible voice. So I broke the silence—but my voice broke, a new voice rose, then came a forgotten voice, the disappeared voice, the voice of freedom, a desperate voice... and through it all, it had all been my voice—the voice that remains."

.

.

.

.

.

.

.

.

.

* Contact me: mycursedgrimoire@gmail.com
* Instagram / Socials : na_z.ar

.

.

.

.

.

Your words matter to me—
Just as mine, I hope, mattered to you.
   With quiet gratitude,
[nazar]